# FÜN學美國各學科

## Preschool 閱讀課本 二版

### AMERICAN SCHOOL TEXTBOOK

# Reading Key

**3**

### Preschool 名詞篇

MP3

寂天雲 APP

作者 ◎ Michael A. Putlack & e-Creative Contents

譯者 ◎ 歐寶妮

## 如何下載 MP3 音檔

❶ 寂天雲 APP 聆聽：掃描書上 QR Code 下載「寂天雲－英日語學習隨身聽」APP。加入會員後，用 APP 內建掃描器再次掃描書上 QR Code，即可使用 APP 聆聽音檔。

❷ 官網下載音檔：請上「寂天閱讀網」（www.icosmos.com.tw），註冊會員／登入後，搜尋本書，進入本書頁面，點選「MP3 下載」下載音檔，存於電腦等其他播放器聆聽使用。

## Authors

### Michael A. Putlack

Michael A. Putlack graduated from Tufts University in Medford, Massachusetts, USA, where he got his B.A. in History and English and his M.A. in History. He has written a number of books for children, teenagers, and adults.

### e-Creative Contents

A creative group that develops English contents and products for ESL and EFL students.

# American School Textbook
# Reading Key – Preschool

## The Best Preparation for Building Basic Vocabulary and Grammar

*The Reading Key — Preschool* series is designed to help children understand basic words and grammar to learn English. This series also helps children develop their reading skills in a fun and easy way.

### Features

- Learning high-frequency words that appear in all kinds of reading material
- Building basic grammar and reading comprehension skills to learn English
- Various activities including reading and writing practice
- A wide variety of topics that cover American school subjects
- Full-color photographs and illustrations

## The Reading Key series has five levels.

○ Reading Key **Preschool 1-6**
a six-book series designed for preschoolers and kindergarteners

○ Reading Key **Basic 1-4**
a four-book series designed for kindergarteners and beginners

○ Reading Key **Volume 1-3**
a three-book series designed for beginner to intermediate learners

○ Reading Key **Volume 4-6**
a three-book series designed for intermediate to high-intermediate learners

○ Reading Key **Volume 7-9**
a three-book series designed for high-intermediate learners

# Table of Contents | Preschool 3 **Nouns**

**Components** **Workbook for Daily Review** • **Answers and Translations**

## Syllabus | Preschool 3 Nouns

| Subject | Unit | Grammar | Vocabulary |
|---|---|---|---|
| **Common Nouns & Usage** | **Unit 1** Animals | Singular and plural Plurals that add "–s" | • a lion, lions<br>• I see a monkey.<br>• I see monkeys. |
| | **Unit 2** Fruits and Vegetables | Using "a" and "an" Plurals that add "–es" | • an apple, apples<br>• a tomato, tomatoes<br>• There is / There are |
| | **Unit 3** My Body | Singular and plural Irregular plurals | • an eye, eyes<br>• foot, feet / tooth, teeth<br>• I have / Do you have? |
| | **Unit 4** Transportation | Demonstrative pronouns 1 | • this, that<br>• This is / That is<br>• Is this? / Is that?<br>• What is this? |
| | **Unit 5** School | Demonstrative pronouns 2 | • this, these<br>• This is / These are<br>• They are<br>• What are these? |
| | **Unit 6** People | Job descriptions | • She is / Is she?<br>• What is she?<br>• What does she do? |
| | **Unit 7** Clothing | Pairs of things | • a skirt, shoes<br>• There is / There are<br>• shoes/socks/pants/shorts<br>• He is wearing / What is he wearing? |
| | **Unit 8** Food | Countable and uncountable nouns | • a hamburger, a sandwich<br>• rice, bread, chicken, ice cream<br>• I like / I don't like<br>• Do you like? |

# Animals
## A Lion, Lions

 **Key Words** Read the words.

 →

a **lion**  **lions**

 →

a **tiger**  **tigers**

 →

a **monkey**  **monkeys**

**a zebra**　　　　　　**zebras**

**a panda**　　　　　　**pandas**

**a snake**　　　　　　**snakes**

# Match Up

Match the words with the pictures.

**one**

**two or more**

- a monkey -
- monkeys -

- a tiger -
- tigers -

- a lion -
- lions -

- a panda -
- pandas -

- a zebra -
- zebras -

- a snake -
- snakes -

# How Many?

Circle the words **in blue**. Underline the words **in red**.

one monkey

two monkeys

one **tiger**

two tigers

one **panda**

three pandas

one zebra

many zebras

I see a (**monkey**, **monkeys**).

I see a (**panda**, **pandas**).

I see a (**tiger**, **tigers**).

I see a (**lion**, **lions**).

I see a (**zebra**, **zebras**).

I see a (**snake**, **snakes**).

# I See Monkeys

Put a check under the correct picture.

I see monkeys.

☐ ☑

I see two pandas.

☐ ☐

I see three lions.

☐ ☐

I see many zebras.

☐ ☐

I see many snakes.

☐ ☐

# I Can Read

Read the story. Look at the pictures.
Circle the correct word or words for each sentence.

**At the Zoo**

Look!
I see (**a tiger**, **tigers**).

Look!
I see (**a lion**, **lions**).

Look!
I see (**a zebra, zebras**).

Look!
I see many (**monkey, monkeys**).

I see many (**panda, pandas**), too.

# Fruits and Vegetables

## An Apple, Apples

 **Key Words** Read the words.

a banana

a tomato

a potato

an apple

an orange

an onion

bananas

apples

oranges

onions

tomatoes

potatoes

15

# Match Up

Match the words with the pictures.

| one | | two or more |
|---|---|---|
| | • an apple •<br>• apples • |  |
|  | • an orange •<br>• oranges • | |
| | • an onion •<br>• onions • |  |
| | • a banana •<br>• bananas • | |
| | • a tomato •<br>• tomatoes • |  |
| | • a potato •<br>• potatoes • | |

**There Is**

Underline the word **is**. (Circle) the correct word for each sentence.

There is <u>is</u> (**a**, (**an**)) apple.

There is (**a**, **an**) orange.

There is (**a**, **an**) onion.

There is (**a**, **an**) banana.

There is (**a**, **an**) tomato.

There is (**a**, **an**) potato.

# There Are

Underline the word **are**. Circle the correct word for each sentence.

There <u>are</u> (**apple**, **apples**).

There are (**orange**, **oranges**).

There are (**onion**, **onions**).

There are (**banana**, **bananas**).

There are (**tomato**, **tomatoes**).

There are (**potato**, **potatoes**).

# One or More?

Put a check under the correct picture.

☑ ☐

There is an apple.

☐ ☐

There are two bananas.

☐ ☐

There is an orange.

☐ ☐

There are three tomatoes.

☐ ☐

There is an onion.

☐ ☐

There are many potatoes.

# I Can Read

Read the story. Find the basket. Follow the path that has the words **There are**.

**Let's Go to the Picnic.**

**Jane**

**There is**

Jane has a basket.

There is an apple in the basket.
There is an orange in the basket.
There is an onion in the basket.

**Tom**

**There are**

Tom has a basket.

There are two potatoes in the basket.
There are three tomatoes in the basket.
There are many bananas in the basket.

*Find and circle Tom's basket.*

**There are**

**There is**

?

?

# My Body
## An Eye, Eyes

**Key Words** Read the words.

eye

nose

ear

mouth

arm

tooth

foot

toe

hand

leg

finger

an **eye**  eye**s**

an **ear**  ear**s**

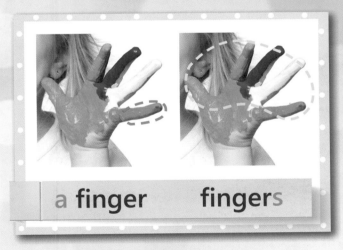

a **finger**  **finger**s

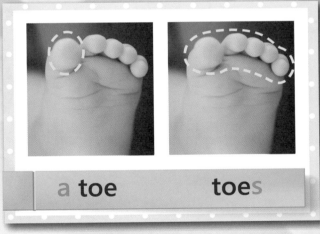

a **toe**  **toe**s

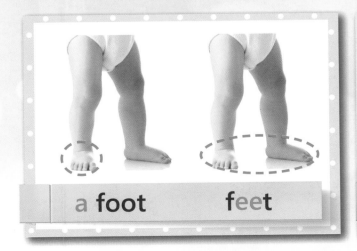

a **foot**  **f**ee**t**

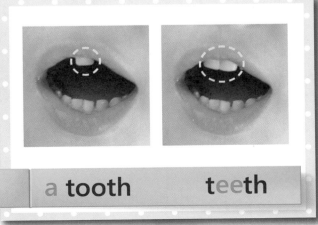

a **tooth**  **t**ee**th**

# Match Up

Match the words with the pictures.

eyes

nose

mouth

ears

teeth

arms

hands

legs

fingers

feet

toes

# An Eye or Eyes?

Circle the correct word or words.

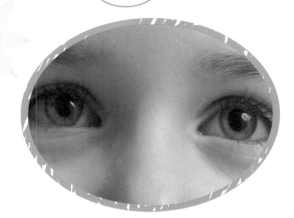

(an eye, eyes)

(an ear, ears)

(a hand, hands)

(a finger, fingers)

(a foot, feet)

(a tooth, teeth)

# I Have

Circle the word **have**. Draw lines to match the sentences with the pictures.

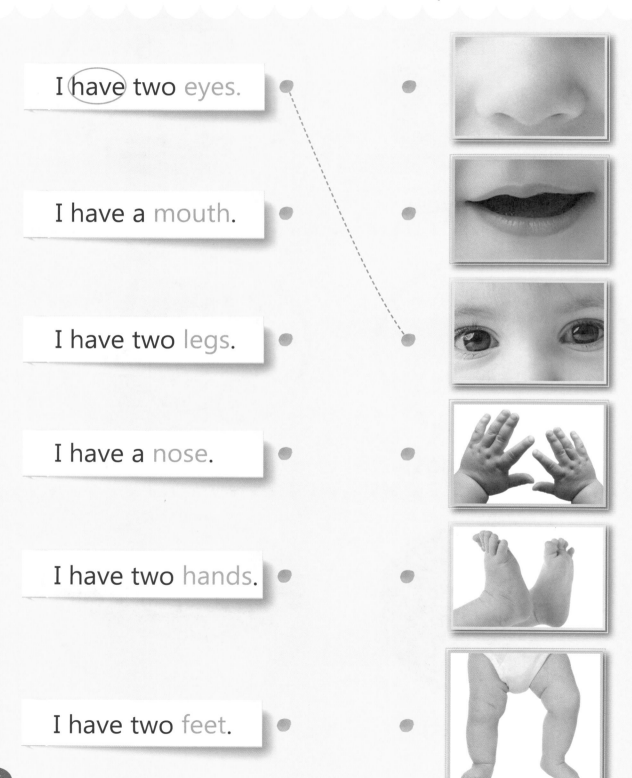

I (have) two eyes.

I have a mouth.

I have two legs.

I have a nose.

I have two hands.

I have two feet.

# Do You Have?

Circle the words **Do you**. Underline the words **Yes** and **No**.

(Do you) have eyes?

Yes, I do.

Do you have ears?

Yes, I do.

Do you have teeth?

Yes, I do.

Do you have fingers?

No, I do not.

Do you have legs?

No, I don't.

# I Can Read

Read the story. (Circle) the word **has**.

Hi!
I am Emily.

This is my sister.

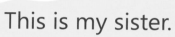

She (has) big eyes.

She has a big nose.

She has a big mouth.

# Transportation
## This, That

 **Key Words** Read the words.

a **car**

a **bus**

a **school bus**

a **truck**

**an airplane**

**a taxi**

**a train**

**a bicycle**

**a motorcycle**

 **Match Up**

Match the words with the pictures.

a car

a school bus

a truck

a taxi

a train

a bicycle

a motorcycle

 an airplane

# This and That

Circle the word **This**. Underline the word **That**.

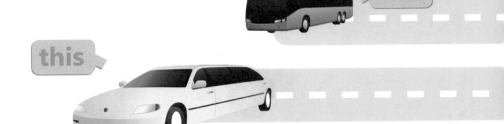

(This) is a car.
That is a bus.

This is a bicycle.
That is a motorcycle.

This is a taxi.
That is a truck.

This is a train.
That is an airplane.

# Is This? Is That?

Circle the words **Is this**. Underline the words **Is that**.

# What Is?

(23)

Circle the sentences **in blue**. Underline the words **It is**.

What is this?
It is a taxi.

What is this?
It is a school bus.

What is that?
It is a bicycle.

What is that?
It is an airplane.

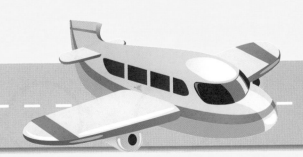

# I Can Read

Read the story. Circle the words **in blue**.

How Do You Go to School?

This is a bus.
I take the bus to school.

This is a bicycle.
I ride my bicycle to school.

This is a train.
I take the train to school.

How do you go to school?
I walk to school!

## Review Test 1

### A Choose and write.

> legs　teeth　eyes　feet　snakes　monkeys　pandas

1. eyes
2.
3.
4.
5.
6.
7.

### B Circle the correct word for each sentence.

1.

There is (**a**, **(an)**) orange.

2.

There is (**a**, **an**) banana.

3.

There is (**a**, **an**) airplane.

4.

There is (**a**, **an**) car.

5.

There are two
(**tomato**, **tomatoes**).

6.

There are many
(**potato**, **potatoes**).

## C Circle the correct word for each sentence.

1.

Is this a train?
Yes, it is.
It is a (train, truck).

2.

Is this a motorcycle?
No, it isn't.
It is a (**motorcycle, bicycle**).

3.

Is that an airplane?
Yes, it is.
It is an (**airplane, bus**).

4.

Is that a bus?
No, it isn't.
It is a (**bus, taxi**).

## D Match the sentences with the pictures.

1. What is this?
It is a tiger.

2. What is this?
It is a zebra.

3. What is that?
It is a motorcycle.

4. What is that?
It is a school bus.

5. What is that?
It is a truck.

# School
## This, These

 **Key Words** Read the words.

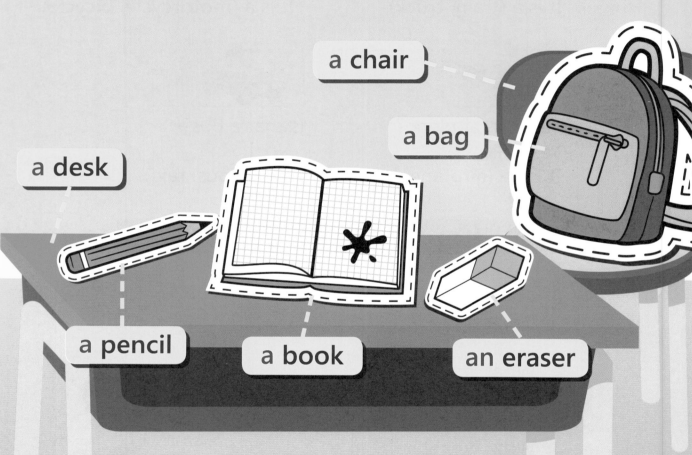

a chair

a bag

a desk

a pencil

a book

an eraser

ABC

a board

a globe

a table

a map

# Match Up

Match the words with the pictures.

a desk

a chair

a table

a book

a pencil

an eraser

a bag

a board

a map

a globe

# This Is

(27)

Circle the correct word for each sentence.

← This is a (**desk**, (**chair**)).

This is a (**table**, **desk**). →

← This is an (**eraser**, **pencil**).

This is a (**book**, **board**). →

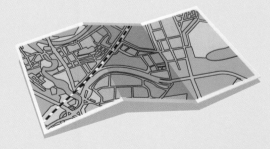

← This is a (**map**, **globe**).

This is a (**globe**, **map**). →

43

# These Are

Circle the words **These are**. Underline the correct word for each sentence.

These are (**desk, desks**).

These are (**chair, chairs**).

These are (**book, books**).

These are (**eraser, erasers**).

These are (**bag, bags**).

These are (**map, maps**).

# What Are These?

Underline the sentence **What are these**?

Circle the word **They**.

What are these?

They are desks.

What are these?

They are chairs.

What are these?

They are bags.

What are these?

They are books.

# I Can Read

Read the story. Answer the questions.

**What is this?**

It is a ( **board**, **book** ).

What is this?

What is this?

It is an ( **eraser**, **chair** ).

What are these?

They are (**desks, tables**).

What are these?

They are (**pencils, pens**).

What are these?

They are (**books, bags**).

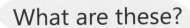

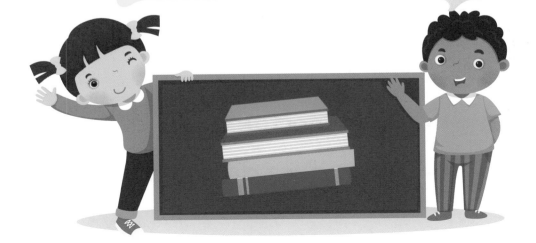

# UNIT 6

# People
## What Is She?

 **Key Words** Read the words.

a teacher

a student

a nurse

a doctor

a firefighter

a police officer

a singer

a dancer

an actor

49

Circle the correct word or words for each sentence.

 She is a (**teacher**, **student**).

He is a (**doctor**, **nurse**).

 She is a (**police officer**, **firefighter**).

He is a (**police officer**, **firefighter**).

 She is a (**singer**, **dancer**).

He is an (**actor**, **dancer**).

# Is She?

Underline the words **Is she** and **Is he**.

Circle the words **is** and **isn't**.

Is she a teacher?

➡ Yes, she is.
She is a teacher.

Is he a police officer?

➡ Yes, he is.
He is a police officer.

Is she a nurse?

➡ No, she isn't.
She is a doctor.

Is he an actor?

➡ No, he isn't.
He is a dancer.

# What Is She?

Circle the sentence **What is she?**

Underline the sentence **What is he?**

 What is she?
 She is a nurse.

 What is she?
 She is a teacher.

 What is he?
 He is a police officer.

 What is he?
 He is a firefighter.

 What is he?
 He is an actor.

# What Does She Do?

Circle the sentences **in blue**. Draw lines to match the sentences with the pictures.

(What does she do?)
She is a student.

What does he do?
He is a nurse.

What does she do?
She is a doctor.

What does he do?
He is a firefighter.

# I Can Read

Read the story. Circle the correct word or words for each sentence.

**This is my family.**

This is my father.
He is a (**teacher**, **doctor**).

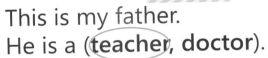

This is my mother.
She is a (**police officer**, **nurse**).

This is my brother.
He is a (**firefighter, dancer**).

This is my sister.
She is a (**student, singer**).

# Clothing
## A Skirt, Shoes

**37** **Key Words** Read the words.

a dress

a skirt

a sweater

a T-shirt

pants

shorts

jeans

pajamas

shoes

boots

socks

# A Shoe or Shoes?

Circle the correct word or words.

(a pant, **pants**)

(a short, shorts)

(a jean, jeans)

(a pajama, pajamas)

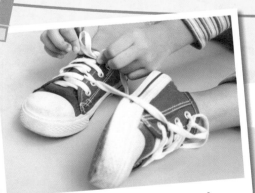

(a shoe, shoes)

(a sock, socks)

# There Is or There Are?

Circle the correct word for each sentence.

There (**is**, **are**) a sweater.

There (**is**, **are**) a dress.

There (**is**, **are**) a T-shirt.

There (**is**, **are**) a skirt.

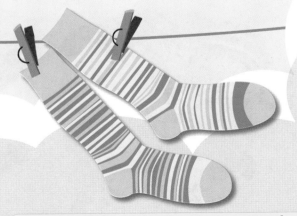

There (**is**, **are**) two shoes.

There (**is**, **are**) two socks.

# He Is Wearing

Circle the words **in blue**.

 She is wearing a dress.

 He is wearing a T-shirt.

 She is wearing jeans.

 He is wearing shorts.

 She is wearing boots.

 He is wearing pajamas.

# What Is He Wearing?

Circle the correct word or words for each sentence.

What is he wearing?

He is wearing (**pants**, **shorts**).

What is she wearing?

She is wearing (**a skirt**, **skirts**).

What is he wearing?

He is wearing (**a shoe**, **shoes**).

What is she wearing?

She is wearing (**a sock**, **socks**).

What is she wearing?

She is wearing (**a pajama**, **pajamas**).

# I Can Read

Read the story. Circle the words **in blue**.

## What Do You Wear?

I wear a uniform to school.

I wear socks to school.

I wear shoes to school.

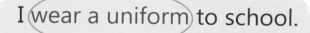

Sometimes I wear rain boots to school.

After school, I wear a T-shirt and shorts.

I wear pajamas **at night**.

# Food
## A Hamburger, Chicken

 **Key Words** Read the words.

a hamburger

a sandwich

rice

bread

chicken

ice cream

milk

orange juice

# A Hamburger or Hamburgers?

Circle the words **in blue**.

a hamburger

a sandwich

hamburgers

sandwiches

rice

rice

bread

bread

chicken

ice cream

chicken

ice cream

# I Like

Circle the word **like**.

I like hamburgers.

I like sandwiches.

I like ice cream.

I like chicken.

I like milk.

I like orange juice.

# I Don't Like

Circle the words **don't like**.

I (don't like) hamburgers.

I don't like chicken.

I don't like rice.

I don't like bread.

I don't like milk.

I don't like ice cream.

# Do You Like?

Circle the correct word for each sentence.

 Do you like sandwiches?

Yes, I do.
I like (**sandwich**, **sandwiches**).

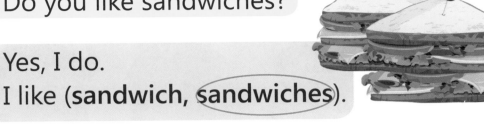

 Do you like hamburgers?

No, I don't.
I don't like (**hamburger**, **hamburgers**).

 Do you like chicken?

Yes, I do.
I like (**chicken**, **chickens**).

 Do you like bread?

No, I don't.
I don't like (**bread**, **breads**).

# I Can Read

Read the story. Circle the words **in blue**.

It's lunchtime!

I eat lunch.
I like sandwiches.

**A** Choose and write.

board   desk   globe   map   shorts   jeans   pants   socks

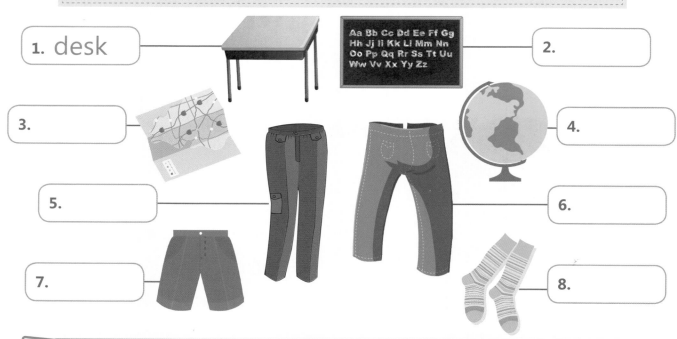

1. desk

2.

3.

4.

5.

6.

7.

8.

**B** Circle the correct word or words for each sentence.

1. What is he wearing?
   He is wearing ( **pants**, (**shorts**) ).

2. What is she wearing?
   She is wearing ( **a dress**, **dresses** ).

3. What is he wearing?
   He is wearing ( **socks**, **shoes** ).

4. What is she wearing?
   She is wearing ( **socks**, **shoes** ).

## C Circle the correct word for each sentence.

1.
What is this?
It is an ( **eraser**, erasers ).

2.
What is this?
It is a ( **table**, tables ).

3.
What are these?
They are ( sandwich, **sandwiches** ).

4.
What are these?
They are ( **hamburgers**, hamburger ).

## D Match the sentences with the pictures.

1. What does she do?
She is a teacher.

2. What does he do?
He is a police officer.

3. What does she do?
She is a doctor.

4. What does he do?
He is a firefighter.

# Word List

## Unit 1

### Animals 動物

**A Lion, Lions** 一隻獅子，很多隻獅子

| 1 | **a lion** | 一隻獅子 |
| 2 | **lions** | 很多隻獅子 |
| 3 | **a tiger** | 一隻老虎 |
| 4 | **tigers** | 很多隻老虎 |
| 5 | **a monkey** | 一隻猴子 |
| 6 | **monkeys** | 很多隻猴子 |
| 7 | **a zebra** | 一隻斑馬 |
| 8 | **zebras** | 很多隻斑馬 |
| 9 | **a panda** | 一隻貓熊 |
| 10 | **pandas** | 很多隻貓熊 |
| 11 | **a snake** | 一條蛇 |
| 12 | **snakes** | 很多條蛇 |
| 13 | **one** | 一；一個 |
| 14 | **two** | 二；兩個 |
| 15 | **or** | 或者 |
| 16 | **more** | 更多的 |
| 17 | **three** | 三；三個 |
| 18 | **many** | 許多的 |
| 19 | **see** | 看見 |
| 20 | **I see** | 我看見…… |
| 21 | **at** | 在……（地點） |
| 22 | **zoo** | 動物園 |
| 23 | **at the zoo** | 在動物園 |
| 24 | **look** | 看 |
| 25 | **too** | 也 |

## Unit 2

### Fruits and Vegetables
水果和蔬菜

**An Apple, Apples**
一顆蘋果，很多顆蘋果

| 1 | **a banana** | 一根香蕉 |
| 2 | **bananas** | 很多根香蕉 |
| 3 | **a tomato** | 一顆番茄 |
| 4 | **tomatoes** | 很多顆番茄 |
| 5 | **a potato** | 一顆馬鈴薯 |

| | | | |
|---|---|---|---|
| 6 | potatoes | 很多顆馬鈴薯 | |
| 7 | an apple | 一顆蘋果 | |
| 8 | apples | 很多顆蘋果 | |
| 9 | an orange | 一顆橘子 | |
| 10 | oranges | 很多顆橘子 | |
| 11 | an onion | 一顆洋蔥 | |
| 12 | onions | 很多顆洋蔥 | |
| 13 | There is | 有……（單數用） | |
| 14 | There are | 有……（複數用） | |
| 15 | Let's | 讓我們…… | |
| 16 | go to | 去…… | |
| 17 | picnic | 野餐 | |

18 **Let's go to the picnic.**
我們去野餐吧。

| | | | |
|---|---|---|---|
| 19 | basket | 籃子 | |
| 20 | in | 在……裡面 | |
| 21 | in the basket | 在籃子裡面 | |
| 22 | Find | 找到 | |
| 23 | Tom's basket | 湯姆的籃子 | |

## Unit 3

# My Body 我的身體
**An Eye, Eyes** 一隻眼睛，很多隻眼睛

| | | | |
|---|---|---|---|
| 1 | an eye | 一隻眼睛 | |
| 2 | eyes | 很多隻眼睛 | |
| 3 | an ear | 一隻耳朵 | |

| | | | |
|---|---|---|---|
| 4 | ears | 很多隻耳朵 | |
| 5 | a nose | 一個鼻子 | |
| 6 | a mouth | 一張嘴 | |
| 7 | an arm | 一隻手臂 | |
| 8 | arms | 很多隻手臂 | |
| 9 | a finger | 一隻手指 | |
| 10 | fingers | 很多隻手指 | |
| 11 | a hand | 一隻手 | |
| 12 | hands | 很多隻手 | |
| 13 | a leg | 一條腿 | |
| 14 | legs | 很多條腿 | |
| 15 | a toe | 一根腳趾 | |
| 16 | toes | 很多根腳趾 | |
| 17 | a foot | 一隻腳 | |
| 18 | feet | 很多隻腳 | |
| 19 | a tooth | 一顆牙齒 | |
| 20 | teeth | 很多顆牙齒 | |
| 21 | have | 有 | |
| 22 | I have | 我有…… | |
| 23 | two eyes | 兩隻眼睛 | |
| 24 | two hands | 兩隻手 | |
| 25 | two legs | 兩條腿 | |
| 26 | two feet | 兩隻腳 | |
| 27 | **Do you have . . . ?** | | 你有……嗎? |

28 **Do you have eyes?**
你有眼睛嗎?

| 29 | **Yes, I do.** | 是的，我有。 |
|----|----|----|
| 30 | **No, I do not. (=No, I don't.)** 不，我沒有。 | |
| 31 | **This is** | 這是…… |
| 32 | **sister** | 姐妹 |
| 33 | **This is my sister.** 這是我的姐妹。 | |
| 34 | **has** | 有 |
| | *he, she, it 他；她；它 | |
| 35 | **big** | 大的 |
| 36 | **She has big eyes.** 她有一雙大眼睛。 | |
| 37 | **long** | 長的 |
| 38 | **She has long legs.** 她有一雙長腿。 | |
| 39 | **tall** | 高的 |
| 40 | **pretty** | 漂亮的 |

## Unit 4

# Transportation 運輸工具

This, That 這個，那個

| 1 | **a car** | 一輛車 |
|----|----|----|
| 2 | **a bus** | 一輛巴士 |
| 3 | **a school bus** | 一輛校車 |
| 4 | **a truck** | 一輛卡車 |
| 5 | **a taxi** | 一輛計程車 |
| 6 | **a train** | 一列火車 |

| 7 | **an airplane** | 一架飛機 |
|----|----|----|
| 8 | **a bicycle** | 一台腳踏車 |
| 9 | **a motorcycle** | 一台摩托車 |
| 10 | **this** | 這個 |
| 11 | **that** | 那個 |
| 12 | **This is** | 這是…… |
| 13 | **That is** | 那是…… |
| 14 | **Is this...?** | 這是……嗎？ |
| 15 | **Is that...?** | 那是……嗎？ |
| 16 | **Is this a car?** | 這是一輛車嗎？ |
| 17 | **Yes, it is.** | 是，它是。 |
| 18 | **No, it isn't.** | 不，它不是。 |
| 19 | **What is this?** | 這是什麼？ |
| 20 | **It is a taxi.** | 它是一輛計程車。 |
| 21 | **What is that?** | 那是什麼？ |
| 22 | **how** | 如何 |
| 23 | **go to school** | 去學校 |
| 24 | **How do you go to school?** 你如何去學校？ | |
| 25 | **take** | 搭乘 |
| 26 | **take the bus** | 搭乘公車 |
| 27 | **ride** | 騎乘 |
| 28 | **ride my bicycle** | 騎我的腳踏車 |
| 29 | **take the train** | 搭乘火車 |
| 30 | **walk** | 走路 |

## Unit 5

# School 學校
### This, These 這個，這些

1. **a desk** 一張書桌
2. **desks** 很多張書桌
3. **a chair** 一張椅子
4. **chairs** 很多張椅子
5. **a table** 一張桌子
6. **tables** 很多張桌子
7. **a bag** 一個包包
8. **bags** 很多個包包
9. **a book** 一本書
10. **books** 很多本書
11. **a pencil** 一枝鉛筆
12. **pencils** 很多枝鉛筆
13. **an eraser** 一塊橡皮擦
14. **erasers** 很多塊橡皮擦
15. **a board** 一塊黑板
16. **boards** 很多塊黑板
17. **a map** 一張地圖
18. **maps** 很多張地圖
19. **a globe** 一顆地球儀
20. **globes** 很多顆地球儀
21. **This is** 這是……
22. **These are** 這些是……
23. **What are these?** 這些是什麼？
24. **They are** 它們是……
25. **They are desks.** 它們是書桌。

## Unit 6

# People 人們
### What Is She? 她的職業是什麼？

1. **a teacher** 一位老師
2. **a student** 一位學生
3. **a doctor** 一位醫生
4. **a nurse** 一位護士
5. **a police officer** 一位警察
6. **a firefighter** 一位消防員
7. **a singer** 一位歌手
8. **a dancer** 一位舞者
9. **an actor** 一位演員
10. **She is** 她是……
11. **Is she...?** 她是……嗎？
12. **Is she a teacher?** 她是老師嗎？
13. **Yes, she is.** 對，她是。
14. **No, she isn't.** 不，她不是。
15. **What is she?** 她的職業是什麼？
16. **What does she do?** 她是做什麼的？
17. **my** 我的

| | | |
|---|---|---|
| 18 | **my family** | 我的家人 |
| 19 | **my father** | 我的爸爸 |
| 20 | **my mother** | 我的媽媽 |
| 21 | **my brother** | 我的兄弟 |
| 22 | **my sister** | 我的姐妹 |

## Unit 7

# Clothing 衣物

**A Skirt, Shoes** 一件裙子，很多鞋子

| | | |
|---|---|---|
| 1 | **a dress** | 一件洋裝 |
| 2 | **a skirt** | 一條裙子 |
| 3 | **a sweater** | 一件毛衣 |
| 4 | **a T-shirt** | 一件T恤 |
| 5 | **pants** | 褲子；寬鬆的長褲 |
| 6 | **shorts** | 短褲 |
| 7 | **jeans** | 牛仔褲 |
| 8 | **pajamas** | 睡衣 |
| 9 | **shoes** | 鞋子 |
| 10 | **boots** | 靴子 |
| 11 | **socks** | 襪子 |
| 12 | **wear** | 穿 |
| 13 | **He is wearing jeans.** 他穿著牛仔褲。 | |
| 14 | **What is he wearing?** 他穿著什麼？ | |

| | | |
|---|---|---|
| 15 | **What do you wear?** 你穿什麼？ | |
| 16 | **I wear** | 我穿著…… |
| 17 | **a uniform** | 一件制服 |
| 18 | **sometimes** | 偶爾；有時候 |
| 19 | **rain boots** | 雨靴 |
| 20 | **after school** | 放學後 |
| 21 | **at night** | 在晚上 |

## Unit 8

# Food 食物

**A Hamburger, Chicken**
一個漢堡，雞肉

| | | |
|---|---|---|
| 1 | **a hamburger** | 一個漢堡 |
| 2 | **hamburgers** | 很多個漢堡 |
| 3 | **a sandwich** | 一個三明治 |
| 4 | **sandwiches** | 很多個三明治 |
| 5 | **rice** | 米飯 |
| 6 | **bread** | 麵包 |
| 7 | **chicken** | 雞肉 |
| 8 | **ice cream** | 冰淇淋 |
| 9 | **milk** | 牛奶 |
| 10 | **orange juice** | 柳橙汁 |
| 11 | **like** | 喜歡 |

12  **I like hamburgers.**
我喜歡漢堡。

13  **I don't like hamburgers.**
我不喜歡漢堡。

14  **Do you like sandwiches?**
你喜歡三明治嗎?

15  **Yes, I do.**　　對,我喜歡。

16  **No, I don't.**　　不,我不喜歡。

17  **lunchtime**　　午餐時間

18  **It's lunchtime.**　現在是午餐時間。

19  **lunch**　　　　午餐

20  **I eat lunch.**　我吃午餐。

21  **bread and milk**　麵包和牛奶

國家圖書館出版品預行編目資料

Fun 學美國各學科 Preschool 閱讀課本．3, 名詞篇（寂天隨身聽 APP 版）/
Michael A. Putlack, e-Creative Contents 著 ; 歐寶妮譯．-- 二版．
-- ［臺北市］：
寂天文化，2024.04
　　面；　　公分
ISBN 978-626-300-249-4（菊 8K 平裝）

1.CST: 英語 2.CST: 名詞
805.162　　　　　　　　　　　　　　　113004568

# FÜN學 美國各學科
## Preschool 閱讀課本 3 二版

Preschool 名詞篇

| | |
|---|---|
| 作　　者 | Michael A. Putlack & e-Creative Contents |
| 譯　　者 | 歐寶妮 |
| 編　　輯 | 呂敏如／歐寶妮 |
| 主　　編 | 丁宥暄 |
| 內文排版 | 洪伊珊 |
| 封面設計 | 林書玉 |
| 製程管理 | 洪巧玲 |
| 發 行 人 | 黃朝萍 |
| 出 版 者 | 寂天文化事業股份有限公司 |
| 電　　話 | 02-2365-9739 |
| 傳　　真 | 02-2365-9835 |
| 網　　址 | www.icosmos.com.tw |
| 讀者服務 | onlineservice@icosmos.com.tw |
| 出版日期 | 2024 年 04 月　二版二刷　（寂天雲隨身聽 APP 版） |

郵撥帳號　　1998620-0　　寂天文化事業股份有限公司
訂書金額未滿 1000 元，請外加運費 100 元。
〔若有破損，請寄回更換，謝謝〕

# FÜN學美國各學科
## Preschool 閱讀課本 二版

## AMERiCAN SCHOOL TEXTBOOK
# Reading Key

### 3

> Preschool
> 名詞篇

# WORKBOOK
# 練習本

# Workbook

# Animals
## A Lion, Lions

**A** Read and write.

1.  monkeys
   monkeys

2. zebras
   zebras

3. pandas
   pandas

4. tigers
   tigers

**B** Match and write.

1. one lion     one lion
2. one panda    one panda

3. two tigers   two tigers
4. two snakes   two snakes

5. a zebra      a zebra
6. a monkey     a monkey

## C Circle the correct word for each sentence.

1.

I see a ( **snake**, **snakes** ).

2.

I see a ( **tiger, tigers** ).

3.

I see two ( **monkey, monkeys** ).

4.

I see two ( **zebra, zebras** ).

## D Choose and write.

| pandas | many | two | snake |
|---|---|---|---|

1.

Look!
I see a ___**snake**___ .

2.

Look!
I see _____ lions.

3.

Look!
I see three _____.

4.

Look!
I see _____ zebras.

# 2 Fruits and Vegetables

## An Apple, Apples

### A Read and write.

1.  apples

apples

2.  oranges

oranges

3.  tomatoes

tomatoes

4.  potatoes

potatoes

### B Match and write.

• 1. a banana    a banana    •

• 2. a tomato    a tomato    •

• 3. an apple    an apple    •

• 4. an orange    an orange    •

• 5. an onion    an onion    •

• 6. a potato    a potato    •

**Circle the correct word for each sentence.**

1.

There ( **is**, **are** ) an apple.

2.

There ( **is, are** ) two bananas.

3.

There ( **is, are** ) an orange.

4.

There ( **is, are** ) three tomatoes.

**D** **Choose and write.**

**a**

**an**

1.

**banana**
_____

banana

orange

onion

apple

tomato

potato

2.

_____

3.

_____

4.

_____

5.

_____

6.

_____

# 3 My Body
### An Eye, Eyes

## A Read and write.

1.  hands

hands

2.  fingers

fingers

3.  feet

feet

4. 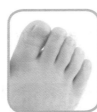 toes

toes

## B Match and write.

1. eyes    eyes

2. ears    ears

3. mouth   mouth

4. nose    nose

5. teeth    teeth

6. legs    legs

**Circle the correct word for each sentence.**

1.
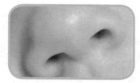
I have a ( **mouth**, (**nose**) ).

2.

I have two ( **hand**, **hands** ).

3.
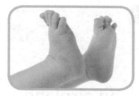
I have two ( **foot**, **feet** ).

4.
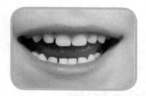
I have many ( **tooth**, **teeth** ).

D **Put a check under the correct picture.**

**Who Am I?**

1. Do you have legs?
No, I don't.

✓      ☐

2. Do you have teeth?
Yes, I do.

☐      ☐

3. Do you have feet?
No, I don't.

  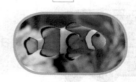

☐      ☐

4. Do you have fingers?
Yes, I do.

☐      ☐

# Transportation

**This, That**

## A Read and write.

1.

a truck

*a truck*

2.

a taxi

*a taxi*

3.

a train

*a train*

4.

an airplane

*an airplane*

## B Match and write.

• 1. a car     *a car* •

• 2. a bus     *a bus* •

• 3. a school bus    *a school bus* •

• 4. a bicycle    *a bicycle* •

• 5. a motorcycle   *a motorcycle* •

## C Circle the correct word for each sentence.

1.

Is this a motorcycle?
➡ Yes, it is.
  It is a ( **bicycle,** (**motorcycle**) ).

2.

Is this a truck?
➡ No, it isn't.
  It is a ( **truck, taxi** ).

3.

Is that a train?
➡ Yes, it is.
  It is a ( **train, airplane** ).

4.

Is that a school bus?
➡ No, it isn't.
  It is a ( **school bus, bus** ).

## D Match the sentences with each picture.

1. What is this?
   It is a school bus.

2. What is this?
   It is a truck.

3. What is that?
   It is a bicycle.

4. What is that?
   It is an airplane.

# School
## This, These

---

### A. Read and write.

1.
a desk

a desk

2.
a table

a table

3.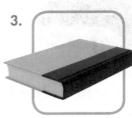
a book

a book

4.
a bag

a bag

---

### B. Match and write.

1. a pencil   a pencil

2. an eraser   an eraser

3. a board   a board

4. a map   a map

5. a globe   a globe

6. a chair   a chair

Circle the correct words for each sentence.

1.

( **This is**, **These are** ) a bag.

2.

( **This is**, **These are** ) a board.

3.

( **This is**, **These are** ) desks.

4.

( **This is**, **These are** ) chairs.

D Match the sentences with each picture.

1. What is this?
It is a desk.

2. What are these?
They are desks.

3. What is this?
It is a book.

4. What are these?
They are books.

5. What are these?
They are globes.

# 6 People

**What Is She?**

## A Read and write.

**1.**

a teacher

a teacher

**2.**

a student

a student

**3.**

a police officer

a police officer

**4.**

a firefighter

a firefighter

## B Match and write.

1. a doctor    a doctor •

2. a nurse    a nurse •

3. a singer    a singer •

4. a dancer    a dancer •

5. an actor    an actor •

## C Circle the correct word or words for each sentence.

**1.**

Is she a student?
➡ Yes, she is.
She is a ( (student), teacher ).

**2.**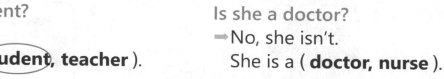

Is she a doctor?
➡ No, she isn't.
She is a ( **doctor, nurse** ).

**3.**

Is he a police officer?
➡ Yes, he is.
He is a ( **police officer, firefighter** ).

**4.**

Is he a singer?
➡ No, he isn't.
He is a ( **singer, firefighter** ).

## D Match the sentences with each picture.

1. What is she?
   She is a teacher. - - - - - - - - - - - -

2. What is he?
   He is an actor.

3. What does she do?
   She is a doctor.

4. What does he do?
   He is a dancer.

15

# Clothing

**A Skirt, Shoes**

 **Read and write.**

1.  a sweater

_a sweater_

2.  a skirt

_a skirt_

3.  pants

_pants_

4.  shorts

_shorts_

**B Match and write.**

• 1. a dress    _a dress_

• 2. a T-shirt    _a T-shirt_  •

• 3. jeans    _jeans_  •

• 4. pajamas    _pajamas_  •

• 5. shoes    _shoes_  •

• 6. boots    _boots_  •

• 7. socks    _socks_  •

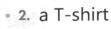

## C Circle the correct word for each sentence.

1. She is wearing ( **a dress**, **dresses** ).

2. He is wearing ( **a T-shirt**, **T-shirts** ).

3. She is wearing ( **a jean**, **jeans** ).

4. He is wearing ( **a short**, **shorts** ).

## D Match the sentences with each picture.

1. What is she wearing?
   She is wearing a skirt.

2. What is he wearing?
   He is wearing shoes.

3. What is she wearing?
   She is wearing socks.

4. What is she wearing?
   She is wearing pajamas.

5. What is he wearing?
   He is wearing pants.

# Food
## A Hamburger, Chicken

### A Read and write.

1.

a hamburger

*a hamburger*

2.

a sandwich

*a sandwich*

3.

chicken

*chicken*

4.

ice cream

*ice cream*

### B Match and write.

- 1. milk          *milk*
- 2. bread         *bread*
- 3. rice          *rice*
- 4. orange juice  *orange juice*
- 5. hamburgers    *hamburgers*
- 6. sandwiches    *sandwiches*

## C Circle the correct word for each sentence.

1.

I like ( **hamburger,** (**hamburgers** )).

2. I like ( **sandwich, sandwiches** ).

3.

I don't like ( **bread, breads** ).

4.

I don't like ( **chicken, chickens** ).

## D Choose and write.

| hamburgers | orange juice | ice cream | rice |

1.

Do you like ice cream?
➡ Yes, I do.
   I like __ice cream__ .

2.

Do you like hamburgers?
➡ No, I don't.
   I don't like _____.

3.

Do you like rice?
➡ Yes, I do.
   I like _____.

4.

Do you like orange juice?
➡ No, I don't.
   I don't like _____.

Textbook
Answers
and
Translations

課本解答與翻譯

# UNIT 1

## Animals 動物
### A Lion, Lions 一隻獅子；很多隻獅子

**Key Words** 關鍵字彙
閱讀以下字詞。

**a lion** 一隻獅子 → **lions** 很多隻獅子

**a tiger** 一隻老虎 → **tigers** 很多隻老虎

**a monkey** 一隻猴子 → **monkeys** 很多隻猴子

**a zebra** 一隻斑馬 → **zebras** 很多隻斑馬

**a panda** 一隻貓熊 → **pandas** 很多隻貓熊

**a snake** 一條蛇 → **snakes** 很多條蛇

**Match Up** 連連看
將圖片連接到正確的字詞。

one 一個 　　 two or more 兩個或更多

a monkey / monkeys 一隻猴子 / 很多隻猴子

a tiger / tigers 一隻老虎 / 很多隻老虎

a lion / lions 一隻獅子 / 很多隻獅子

a panda / pandas 一隻貓熊 / 很多隻貓熊

a zebra / zebras 一隻斑馬 / 很多隻斑馬

a snake / snakes 一條蛇 / 很多條蛇

**How Many?** 多少？
圈出藍色的單字。在紅色單字底下畫線。

one monkey 一隻猴子 　 two monkeys 兩隻猴子

one tiger 一隻老虎 　 two tigers 兩隻老虎

one panda 一隻貓熊 　 three pandas 三隻貓熊

one zebra 一隻斑馬 　 many zebras 很多隻斑馬

## I See a Monkey 我看見一隻猴子
圈出每個句子中正確的單字。

I see a (**monkey**, monkeys).
我看見一隻（猴子；很多猴子）。

I see a (**panda**, pandas).
我看見一隻（貓熊；很多貓熊）

I see a (**tiger**, tigers).
我看見一隻（老虎；很多老虎）。

I see a (**lion**, lions).
我看見一隻（獅子；很多獅子）。

I see a (**zebra**, zebras).
我看見一隻（斑馬；很多斑馬）。

I see a (**snake**, snakes).
我看見一隻（蛇；很多蛇）

10

## I See Monkeys 我看見很多猴子
在正確的圖片底下打勾。

I see monkeys.
我看見很多猴子。

I see two pandas.
我看見兩隻貓熊。

I see three lions.
我看見三隻獅子。

I see many zebras.
我看見很多斑馬。

I see many snakes.
我看見很多蛇。

11

## I Can Read 我會閱讀
閱讀故事，並圈出每個句子中正確的字詞。

**At the Zoo**
在動物園

Look!
I see (**a tiger**, tigers).
看！
我看見（一隻老虎；很多老虎）。

Look!
I see (**a zebra**, zebras).
看！
我看見（一隻斑馬；很多斑馬）。

Look!
I see (**a lion**, lions).
看！
我看見（一隻獅子；很多獅子）。

Look!
I see many (monkey, **monkeys**).
看！
我看見很多（一隻猴子；猴子）。

I see many (panda, **pandas**), too.
我也看見很多（一隻貓熊；貓熊）。

12    13

23

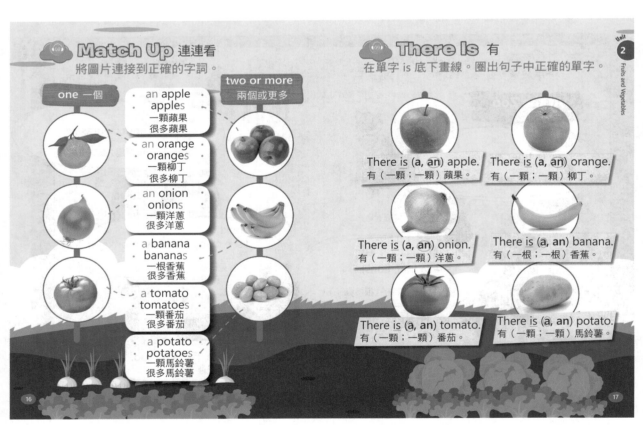

在單字 are 底下畫線。圈出每個句子中正確的單字。

在正確的圖片底下打勾。

Unit 2 Fruits and Vegetables

 There <u>are</u> (apple, **apples**).
有很多蘋果。

There <u>are</u> (orange, **oranges**).
有很多柳丁。

 There <u>are</u> (onion, **onions**).
有很多洋蔥。

There <u>are</u> (banana, **bananas**).
有很多香蕉。

There <u>are</u> (tomato, **tomatoes**).
有很多番茄。

There <u>are</u> (potato, **potatoes**).
有很多馬鈴薯。

☑ ☐    ☐ ☑

There is an apple.
有一顆蘋果。

There are two bananas.
有兩根香蕉。

☐ ☑    ☐ ☑

There is an orange.
有一顆柳丁。

There are three tomatoes.
有三顆番茄。

☑ ☐    ☑ ☐

There is an onion.
有一顆洋蔥。

There are many potatoes.
有很多馬鈴薯。

18

19

---

# I Can Read 我會閱讀

閱讀故事，跟著字詞 There are 的路線找出籃子。

**Let's Go to the Picnic.**
我們去野餐吧。

Jane
珍

**There is** 有

Jane has a basket.
珍有一個籃子。
There is an apple in the basket.
There is an orange in the basket.
There is an onion in the basket.
籃子裡有一顆蘋果。
籃子裡有一顆柳丁。
籃子裡有一顆洋蔥。

Unit 2 Fruits and Vegetables

Tom
湯姆

**There are** 有

Tom has a basket.
湯姆有一個籃子。
There are two potatoes in the basket.
There are three tomatoes in the basket.
There are many bananas in the basket.
籃子裡有兩顆馬鈴薯。
籃子裡有三顆番茄。
籃子裡有很多香蕉。

***Find and circle Tom's basket.***
找出湯姆的籃子並圈出來。

**There are** 有

**There is** 有

20

21

25

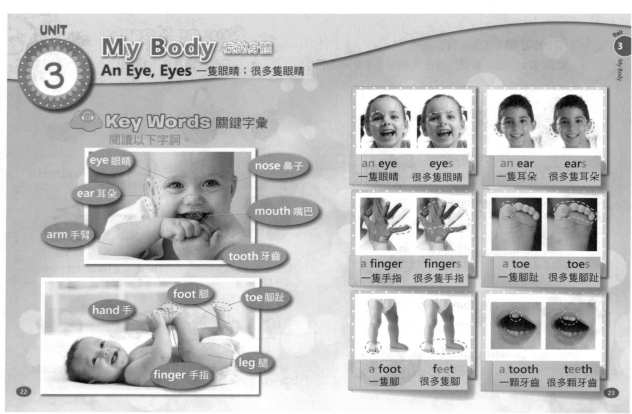

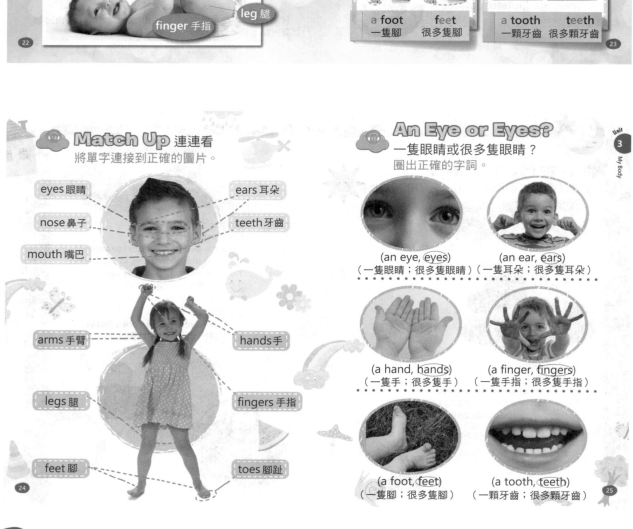

## I Have 我有

圈出單字 have。將句子連接到正確的圖片。

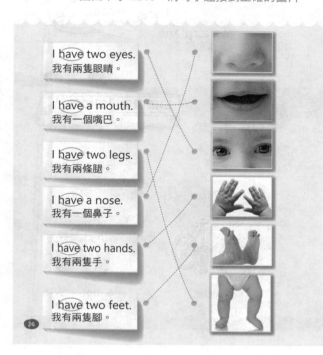

I have two eyes.
我有兩隻眼睛。

I have a mouth.
我有一個嘴巴。

I have two legs.
我有兩條腿。

I have a nose.
我有一個鼻子。

I have two hands.
我有兩隻手。

I have two feet.
我有兩隻腳。

26

## Do You Have? 你有……嗎?

圈出字詞 Do you。在 字詞Yes 和 No 底下畫線。

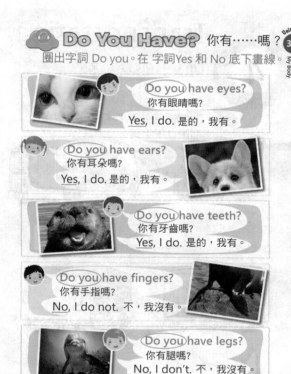

Do you have eyes?
你有眼睛嗎?
Yes, I do. 是的,我有。

Do you have ears?
你有耳朵嗎?
Yes, I do. 是的,我有。

Do you have teeth?
你有牙齒嗎?
Yes, I do. 是的,我有。

Do you have fingers?
你有手指嗎?
No, I do not. 不,我沒有。

Do you have legs?
你有腿嗎?
No, I don't. 不,我沒有。

27

## I Can Read 我會閱讀

閱讀故事,並圈出單字 has。

Hi! 嗨!
I am Emily. 我是愛蜜莉。

This is my sister. 這是我的妹妹。

She has big eyes.
她有一雙大眼睛。

She has a big nose.
她有一個大鼻子。

She has a big mouth.
她有一個大嘴巴。

She has long fingers.
她有長手指。

She has long legs.
她有一雙長腿。

She is tall and pretty!
她又高又美。

28

29

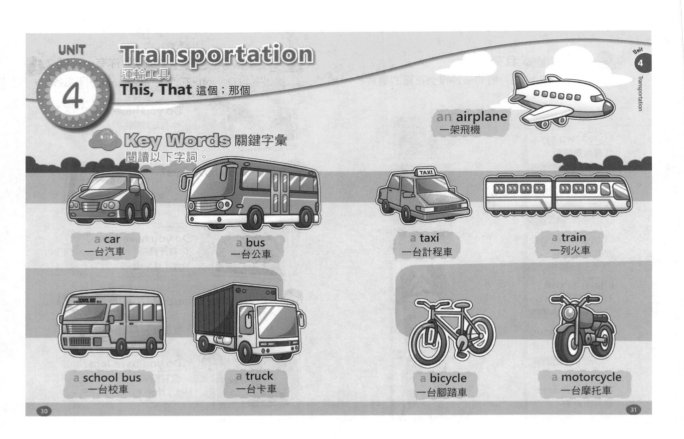

# UNIT 4 Transportation
運輸工具
**This, That** 這個；那個

## Key Words 關鍵字彙
閱讀以下字詞。

an airplane
一架飛機

a car
一台汽車

a bus
一台公車

a taxi
一台計程車

a train
一列火車

a school bus
一台校車

a truck
一台卡車

a bicycle
一台腳踏車

a motorcycle
一台摩托車

## Match Up 連連看
將圖片連接到正確的字詞。

a car
一台汽車
a school bus
一台校車

a truck
一台卡車
a taxi
一台計程車

a train
一列火車
a bicycle
一台腳踏車

a motorcycle
一台摩托車
an airplane
一架飛機

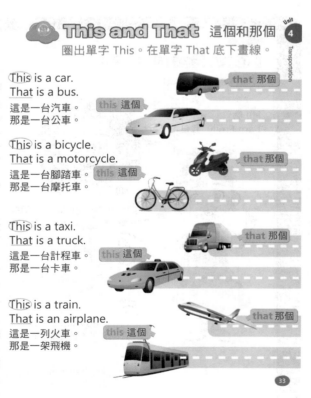

## This and That 這個和那個
圈出單字 This。在單字 That 底下畫線。

This is a car.
That is a bus.
這是一台汽車。
那是一台公車。

that 那個
this 這個

This is a bicycle.
That is a motorcycle.
這是一台腳踏車。
那是一台摩托車。

that 那個
this 這個

This is a taxi.
That is a truck.
這是一台計程車。
那是一台卡車。

that 那個
this 這個

This is a train.
That is an airplane.
這是一列火車。
那是一架飛機。

that 那個
this 這個

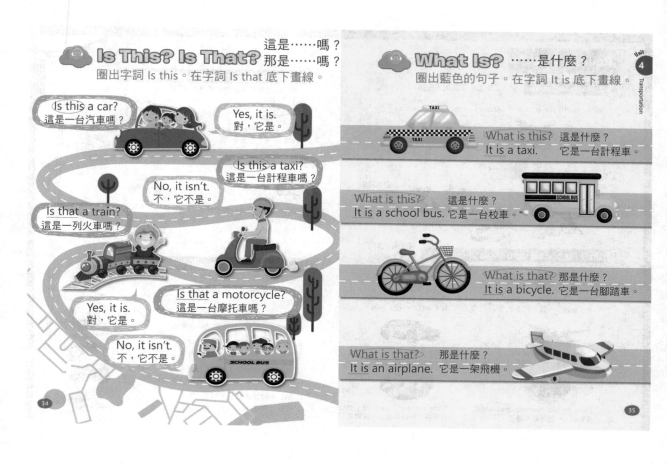

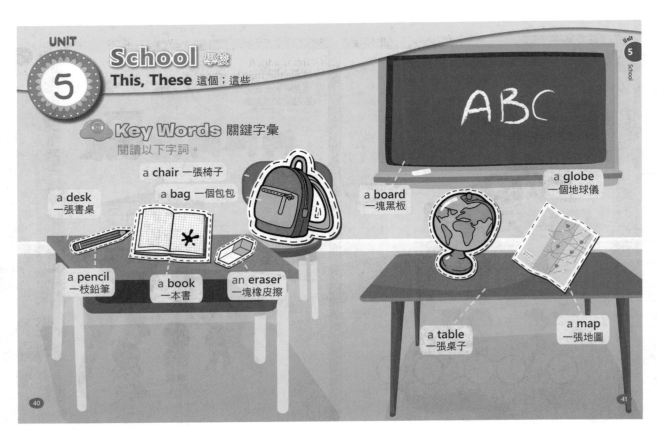

## Match Up 連連看
將圖片連接到正確的字詞。

## This Is 這是
圈出每個句子中正確的單字。

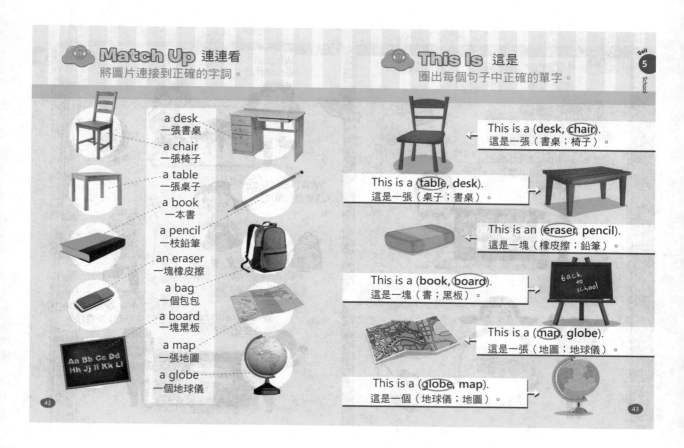

a desk 一張書桌
a chair 一張椅子
a table 一張桌子
a book 一本書
a pencil 一枝鉛筆
an eraser 一塊橡皮擦
a bag 一個包包
a board 一塊黑板
a map 一張地圖
a globe 一個地球儀

This is a (desk, chair).
這是一張（書桌；椅子）。

This is a (table, desk).
這是一張（桌子；書桌）。

This is an (eraser, pencil).
這是一塊（橡皮擦；鉛筆）。

This is a (book, board).
這是一塊（書；黑板）。

This is a (map, globe).
這是一張（地圖；地球儀）。

This is a (globe, map).
這是一個（地球儀；地圖）。

42

43

## These Are 這些是
圈出字詞 These are。在正確的單字底下畫線。

## What Are These? 這些是什麼？
在句子 What are these? 底下畫線。
圈出單字 They。

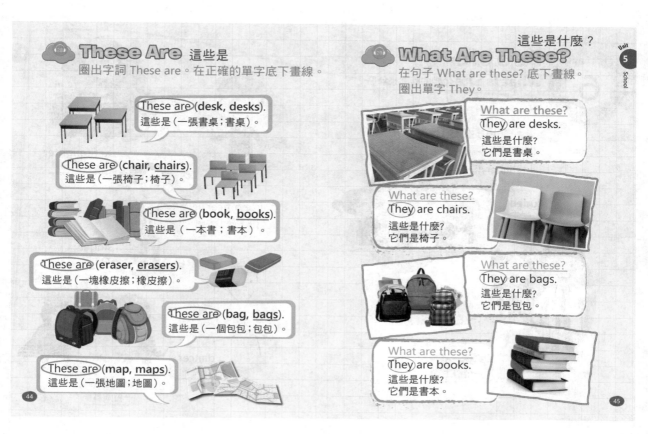

These are (desk, desks).
這些是（一張書桌；書桌）。

These are (chair, chairs).
這些是（一張椅子；椅子）。

These are (book, books).
這些是（一本書；書本）。

These are (eraser, erasers).
這些是（一塊橡皮擦；橡皮擦）。

These are (bag, bags).
這些是（一個包包；包包）。

These are (map, maps).
這些是（一張地圖；地圖）。

What are these?
They are desks.
這些是什麼？
它們是書桌。

What are these?
They are chairs.
這些是什麼？
它們是椅子。

What are these?
They are bags.
這些是什麼？
它們是包包。

What are these?
They are books.
這些是什麼？
它們是書本。

44

45

**I Can Read** 我會閱讀

閱讀故事，並回答問題。

What is this?
這是什麼？

What is this?
這是什麼？

It is a (**board**, book).
它是一塊（黑板；書）。

Aa Bb Cc Dd
Hh Jj Ii Kk L
Oo Pp Qq Rr

What is this?
這是什麼？

It is an (**eraser**, chair).
它是一塊（橡皮擦；椅子）。

What are these?
這些是什麼？

They are (desks, **tables**).
它們是（書桌；桌子）。

What are these?
這些是什麼？

They are (**pencils**, pens).
它們是（鉛筆；筆）。

What are these?
這些是什麼？

They are (**books**, bags).
它們是（書本；包包）。

46

47

## UNIT 6

## People 人們

**What Is She?** 她的職業是什麼？

**Key Words** 關鍵字彙

閱讀以下字詞。

a **teacher**
一位老師

a **student**
一位學生

a **nurse**
一位護士

a **doctor**
一位醫生

a **police officer**
一位警察

a **firefighter**
一位消防員

a **singer**
一位歌手

a **dancer**
一位舞者

an **actor**
一位演員

48

49

**She Is** 她是

圈出每個句子中正確的字詞。

She is a (**teacher**, student).
她是一位（老師；學生）。

He is a (**doctor**, nurse).
他是一位（醫生；護士）。

She is a (police officer, **firefighter**).
她是一位（警察；消防員）。

He is a (**police officer**, firefighter).
他是一位（警察；消防員）。

She is a (**singer**, dancer).
她是一位（歌手；舞者）。

He is an (**actor**, dancer).
他是一位（演員；舞者）。

50

 **Is She?** 她是？

在字詞 Is she 和 Is he 下面畫線。
圈出字詞 is 和 isn't。

Is she a teacher?
她是一位老師嗎？

Yes, she **is**. 對，她是。
She **is** a teacher. 她是一位老師。

Is he a police officer?
他是一位警察嗎？

Yes, he **is**. 對，他是。
He **is** a police officer. 他是一位警察。

Is she a nurse?
她是一位護士嗎？

No, she **isn't**. 不，她不是。
She **is** a doctor. 她是一位醫生。

Is he an actor?
他是一位演員嗎？

No, he **isn't**. 不，他不是。
He **is** a dancer. 他是一位舞者。

51

Unit **6** People

---

 **What Is She?** 她的職業是什麼？

圈出句子 What is she?。在句子 What is he?
底下畫線。

**What is she?**
她的職業是什麼？
She is a nurse.
她是一位護士。

**What is she?**
她的職業是什麼？
She is a teacher.
她是一位老師。

What is he?
他的職業是什麼？
He is a police officer.
他是一位警察。

What is he?
他的職業是什麼？

He is a firefighter.
他是一位消防員。

What is he?
他的職業是什麼？

He is an actor.
他是一位演員。

52

她是做什麼的？
 **What Does She Do?**

圈出藍色的句子。將句子連接到正確
的圖片。

**What does she do?**
She is a student.
她是做什麼的？
她是一名學生。

**What does he do?**
He is a nurse.
他是做什麼的？
他是一名護士。

What does she do?
She is a doctor.
她是做什麼的？
她是一名醫生。

**What does he do?**
He is a firefighter.
他是做什麼的？
他是一名消防員。

53

Unit **6** People

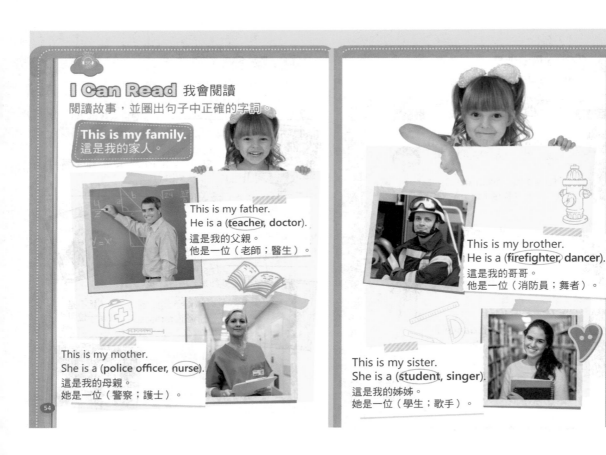

## I Can Read 我會閱讀

閱讀故事，並圈出句子中正確的字詞。

**This is my family.**
這是我的家人。

This is my father.
He is a (**teacher**, doctor).
這是我的父親。
他是一位（老師；醫生）。

This is my mother.
She is a (police officer, **nurse**).
這是我的母親。
她是一位（警察；護士）。

This is my brother.
He is a (**firefighter**, dancer).
這是我的哥哥。
他是一位（消防員；舞者）。

This is my sister.
She is a (**student**, singer).
這是我的姊姊。
她是一位（學生；歌手）。

54

55

## UNIT 7

## Clothing 衣服
### A Skirt, Shoes 一件裙子；很多鞋子

### Key Words 關鍵字彙
閱讀以下字詞。

a dress
一件洋裝

a skirt
一件裙子

a sweater
一件毛衣

a T-shirt
一件T恤

pants
一件長褲

shorts
一件短褲

jeans
一件牛仔褲

pajamas
一套睡衣

shoes
一雙鞋

boots
一雙靴子

socks
一雙襪子

56

57

## A Shoe or Shoes?
一隻鞋或很多鞋？
圈出正確的字詞。

(a pant, **pants**)
（✕；一件長褲）

(a short, **shorts**)
（✕；一件短褲）

(a jean, **jeans**)
（✕；一件牛仔褲）

(a pajama, **pajamas**)
（✕；一套睡衣）

(a shoe, **shoes**)
（一隻鞋；一雙鞋）

(a sock, **socks**)
（一隻襪子；一雙襪子）

58

## There Is or There Are?
有（單數）或有（複數）？
圈出每個句子中正確的單字。

There ( is, **are**) a dress.
有一件洋裝。

There (**is**, are) a sweater.
有一件毛衣。

There (**is**, are) a T-shirt.
有一件T恤。

There (**is**, are) a skirt.
有一件裙子。

There (is, **are**) two shoes.
有一雙鞋。

There (is, **are**) two socks.
有一雙襪子。

59

## He Is Wearing 他穿著
圈出藍色的字詞。

She _is wearing_ a dress.
她穿著洋裝。

He _is wearing_ a T-shirt.
他穿著T恤。

She _is wearing_ jeans.
她穿著牛仔褲。

He _is wearing_ shorts.
他穿著短褲。

She _is wearing_ boots.
她穿著靴子。

He _is wearing_ pajamas.
他穿著睡衣。

60

## What Is He Wearing?
他穿著什麼？
圈出每個句子中正確的字詞。

What is he wearing? 他穿著什麼？
He is wearing (**pants**, shorts).
他穿著（長褲；短褲）。

What is she wearing? 她穿著什麼？
She is wearing (**a skirt**, skirts).
她穿著（一件裙子；很多裙子）。

What is he wearing? 他穿著什麼？
He is wearing (a shoe, **shoes**).
他穿著（一隻鞋；一雙鞋）。

What is she wearing? 她穿著什麼？
She is wearing (a sock, **socks**).
她穿著（一隻襪子；一雙襪子）。

What is she wearing? 她穿著什麼？
She is wearing (a pajama, **pajamas**).
她穿著（✕；睡衣）。

61

35

## A Hamburger or Hamburgers?
一個漢堡或很多個漢堡？
圈出藍色的字詞。

a hamburger 一個漢堡

a sandwich 一個三明治

hamburgers 很多個漢堡

sandwiches 很多個三明治

rice 飯

bread 麵包

rice 很多飯

bread 很多麵包

chicken 雞肉

ice cream 冰淇淋

chicken 很多雞肉

ice cream 很多冰淇淋

66

## I Like 我喜歡
圈出單字 like。

 I like hamburgers.
我喜歡漢堡。

I like sandwiches.
我喜歡三明治。

 I like ice cream.
我喜歡冰淇淋。

I like chicken.
我喜歡雞肉。

 I like milk.
我喜歡牛奶。

I like orange juice.
我喜歡柳橙汁。

Unit 8 Food

67

---

## I Don't Like 我不喜歡
圈出字詞 don't like。

I don't like hamburgers.
我不喜歡漢堡。

I don't like chicken.
我不喜歡雞肉。

I don't like rice.
我不喜歡飯。

I don't like bread.
我不喜歡麵包。

I don't like milk.
我不喜歡牛奶。

I don't like ice cream.
我不喜歡冰淇淋。

68

## Do You Like? 你喜歡……嗎？
圈出每個句子中正確的單字。

 Do you like sandwiches?
你喜歡三明治嗎？

 Yes, I do. 對，我喜歡。
I like (sandwich, sandwiches).
我喜歡三明治。

Do you like hamburgers?
你喜歡漢堡嗎？

No, I don't. 不，我不喜歡。
I don't like (hamburger, hamburgers).
我不喜歡漢堡。

Do you like chicken?
你喜歡雞肉嗎？

Yes, I do. 對，我喜歡。
I like (chicken, chickens).
我喜歡雞肉。

Do you like bread?
你喜歡麵包嗎？

No, I don't. 不，我不喜歡。
I don't like (bread, breads).
我不喜歡麵包。

Unit 8 Food

69

37

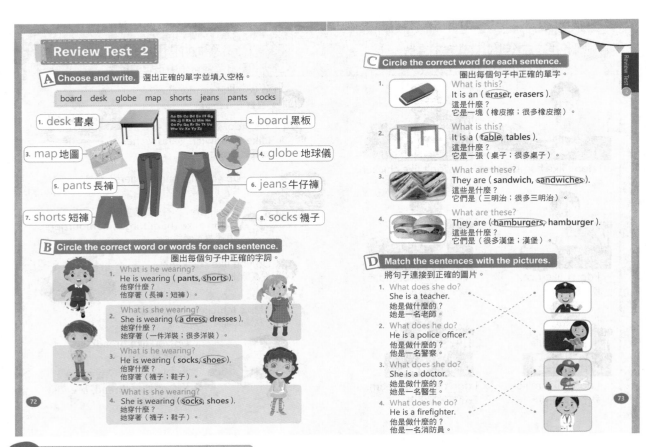

# Daily Test
# Answers

課堂練習解答

# 1 Animals
**A Lion, Lions**

## A Read and write.

1.  monkeys
monkeys

2.  zebras
zebras

3.  pandas
pandas

4.  tigers
tigers

## B Match and write.

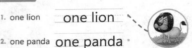

1. one lion — one lion
2. one panda — one panda
3. two tigers — two tigers
4. two snakes — two snakes
5. a zebra — a zebra
6. a monkey — a monkey

## C Circle the correct word for each sentence.

1.  I see a ( **snake**, snakes ).

2.  I see a ( **tiger**, tigers ).

3.  I see two ( **monkey**, **monkeys** ).

4.  I see two ( zebra, **zebras** ).

## D Choose and write.

| pandas | many | two | snake |

1.
Look!
I see a __snake__.

2.
Look!
I see __two__ lions.

3.
Look!
I see three __pandas__.

4.
Look!
I see __many__ zebras.

4

5

---

# 2 Fruits and Vegetables
**An Apple, Apples**

## A Read and write.

1.  apples
apples

2.  oranges
oranges

3.  tomatoes
tomatoes

4.  potatoes
potatoes

## B Match and write.

1. a banana — a banana
2. a tomato — a tomato
3. an apple — an apple
4. an orange — an orange
5. an onion — an onion
6. a potato — a potato

## C Circle the correct word for each sentence.

1.  There ( **is**, are ) an apple.

2.  There ( is, **are** ) two bananas.

3.  There ( **is**, are ) an orange.

4.  There ( is, **are** ) three tomatoes.

## D Choose and write.

**a** | | **an**

1.
**banana**

2.
**orange**

| banana |
| orange |
| onion |
| apple |
| tomato |
| potato |

3.
**tomato**

4.
**onion**

5.
**potato**

6.
**apple**

6

7

---

# 3 My Body
### An Eye, Eyes

**A** Read and write.

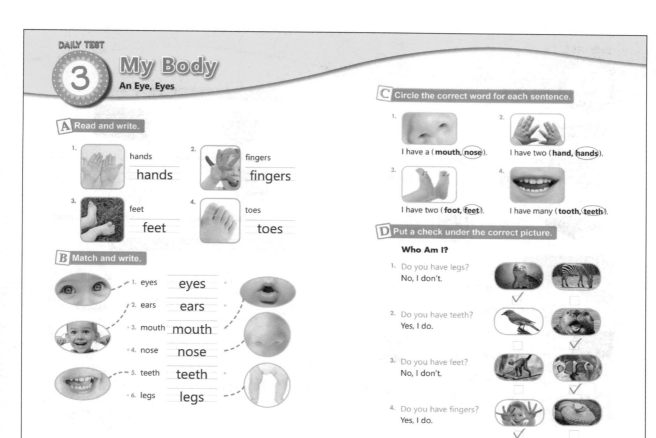

1. hands — hands
2. fingers — fingers
3. feet — feet
4. toes — toes

**B** Match and write.

1. eyes — eyes
2. ears — ears
3. mouth — mouth
4. nose — nose
5. teeth — teeth
6. legs — legs

**C** Circle the correct word for each sentence.

1. I have a ( mouth, (nose) ).
2. I have two ( hand, (hands) ).
3. I have two ( foot, (feet) ).
4. I have many ( tooth, (teeth) ).

**D** Put a check under the correct picture.

**Who Am I?**

1. Do you have legs?
   No, I don't.
2. Do you have teeth?
   Yes, I do.
3. Do you have feet?
   No, I don't.
4. Do you have fingers?
   Yes, I do.

---

# 4 Transportation
### This, That

**A** Read and write.

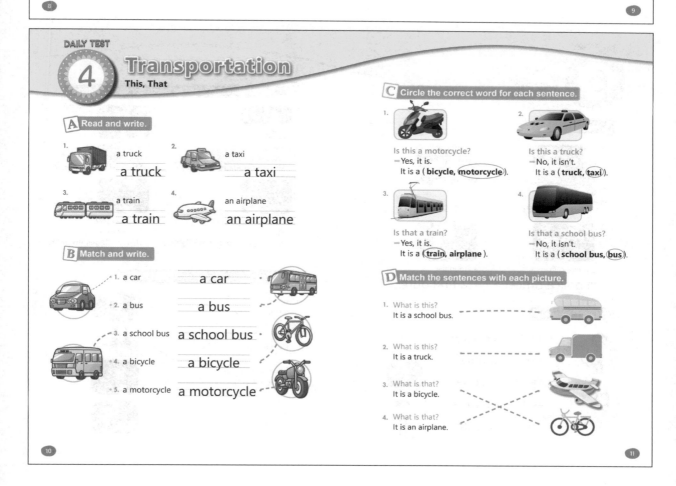

1. a truck — a truck
2. a taxi — a taxi
3. a train — a train
4. an airplane — an airplane

**B** Match and write.

1. a car — a car
2. a bus — a bus
3. a school bus — a school bus
4. a bicycle — a bicycle
5. a motorcycle — a motorcycle

**C** Circle the correct word for each sentence.

1. Is this a motorcycle?
   —Yes, it is.
   It is a ( bicycle, (motorcycle) ).
2. Is this a truck?
   —No, it isn't.
   It is a ( truck, (taxi) ).
3. Is that a train?
   —Yes, it is.
   It is a ( (train), airplane ).
4. Is that a school bus?
   —No, it isn't.
   It is a ( school bus, (bus) ).

**D** Match the sentences with each picture.

1. What is this?
   It is a school bus.
2. What is this?
   It is a truck.
3. What is that?
   It is a bicycle.
4. What is that?
   It is an airplane.

DAILY TEST

# School
**This, These**

## A Read and write.

1.  a desk
a desk

2.  a table
a table

3.  a book
a book

4.  a bag
a bag

## B Match and write.

 • 1. a pencil  a pencil
• 2. an eraser  an eraser
 • 3. a board  a board
• 4. a map  a map
• 5. a globe  a globe
 • 6. a chair  a chair

## C Circle the correct words for each sentence.

1.  ( **This is**, These are ) a bag.
2.  ( **This is**, These are ) a board.
3.  ( This is, **These are** ) desks.
4.  ( This is, **These are** ) chairs.

## D Match the sentences with each picture.

1. What is this?
It is a desk.

2. What are these?
They are desks.

3. What is this?
It is a book.

4. What are these?
They are books.

5. What are these?
They are globes.

12

13

DAILY TEST

# People
**What Is She?**

## A Read and write.

1.  a teacher
a teacher

2. a student
a student

3.  a police officer
a police officer

4.  a firefighter
a firefighter

## B Match and write.

• 1. a doctor  a doctor
• 2. a nurse  a nurse
• 3. a singer  a singer
• 4. a dancer  a dancer
• 5. an actor  an actor

## C Circle the correct word or words for each sentence.

1.  Is she a student?
— Yes, she is.
She is a ( **student**, teacher ).

2.  Is she a doctor?
— No, she isn't.
She is a ( doctor, **nurse** ).

3. Is he a police officer?
— Yes, he is.
He is a ( **police officer**, firefighter ).

4. Is he a singer?
— No, he isn't.
He is a ( singer, **firefighter** ).

## D Match the sentences with each picture.

1. What is she?
She is a teacher.

2. What is he?
He is an actor.

3. What does she do?
She is a doctor.

4. What does he do?
He is a dancer.

14

15

# 7 Clothing
## A Skirt, Shoes

### A Read and write.

1. a sweater

a sweater

2. a skirt

a skirt

3. pants

pants

4. shorts
shorts

### B Match and write.

1. a dress — a dress
2. a T-shirt — a T-shirt
3. jeans — jeans
4. pajamas — pajamas
5. shoes — shoes
6. boots — boots
7. socks — socks

### C Circle the correct word for each sentence.

1. She is wearing ( **a dress**, dresses ).
2. He is wearing ( **a T-shirt**, T-shirts ).

3. She is wearing ( a jean, **jeans** ).
4. He is wearing ( a short, **shorts** ).

### D Match the sentences with each picture.

1. What is she wearing?
She is wearing a skirt.

2. What is he wearing?
He is wearing shoes.

3. What is she wearing?
She is wearing socks.

4. What is she wearing?
She is wearing pajamas.

5. What is he wearing?
He is wearing pants.

16

17

---

# 8 Food
## A Hamburger, Chicken

### A Read and write.

1. a hamburger
a hamburger

2. a sandwich
a sandwich

3. chicken
chicken

4. ice cream
ice cream

### B Match and write.

1. milk — milk
2. bread — bread
3. rice — rice
4. orange juice — orange juice
5. hamburgers — hamburgers
6. sandwiches — sandwiches

### C Circle the correct word for each sentence.

1. I like ( hamburger, **hamburgers** ).
2. I like ( sandwich, **sandwiches** ).

3. I don't like ( **bread**, breads ).
4. I don't like ( **chicken**, chickens ).

### D Choose and write.

| hamburgers | orange juice | ice cream | rice |

1. Do you like ice cream?
— Yes, I do.
I like **ice cream** .

2. Do you like hamburgers?
— No, I don't.
I don't like **hamburgers** .

3. Do you like rice?
— Yes, I do.
I like **rice** .

4. Do you like orange juice?
— No, I don't.
I don't like **orange juice** .

18

19